This book is dedicated to Evie, who has the loudest roar of all.

The Loudest Roar by Clair Maskell

Angus was a very loud lion. His roar was so loud, his Mummy and Daddy were always telling him to "sssh !"
He would roar when he was playing with his brother, roar when he saw his favourite dinner and roar when it was time for bed!

Angus loved to roar. It was such a great sound! However, his roar didn't always work. He wasn't quite sure why, but when Angus left home to go out anywhere, his roar got stuck!

His Mummy and Daddy knew his roar would get stuck, but nobody else could understand.

"Why won't you roar?" the animals at school would ask "Are you shy?" Angus would shake his head. He wanted to answer and tell them that he didn't know why. He wanted to show them just how loud his roar could be, but he just couldn't get it to work, no matter how hard he tried.

Angus loved to play. He liked football and running and dressing up like a superhero. He was brilliant at so many things, but it felt like nobody knew that.

They just worried about his roar.

The teacher at school would ask Angus questions but even though he was clever enough to know the answers, he could never get the words out. He tried his best to answer by pointing and nodding instead.

Even when Angus fell and hurt his head, he couldn't even roar the tiniest roar to show that it hurt. Angus was so, so cross inside.

"My tummy hurts" he roared to his Mummy at home. He wasn't sure why, but all the roars got stuck inside him and made his tummy hurt. All of his biggest roars came out at home until Daddy complained that he had a headache!

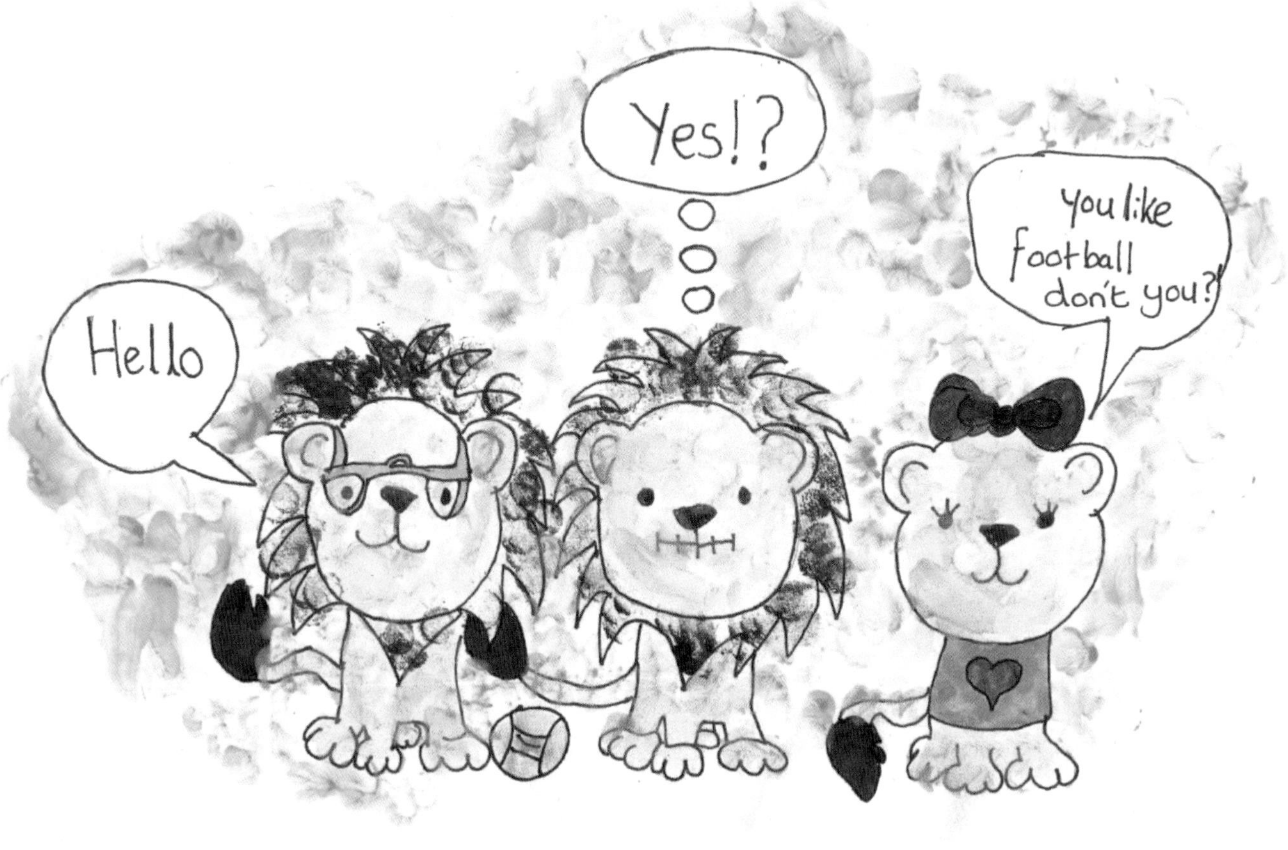
Hello
Yes!?
you like football don't you?

One day at school, Angus was in the playground watching all the animals shouting and chatting and he wished he could join in too.

"Hello" said a voice " You like football, don't you?"
"How did they know that?" Angus wondered

They started to play together. Angus was worried that they would want him to roar, but they didn't even mention it. At last, Angus could play and have fun without worrying about his roar.

He was so pleased to have found friends that could understand that he couldn't roar. They may not have understood why it was that way, but they liked him playing with them. He was roaring inside though. Angus roared the loudest roar inside. It was a roar of happiness.

You couldn't hear it, but it was there

## About the author

Clair Maskell comes from a childcare background. After working with children for over 11 years and completing her degree in childcare and education, she became a full time Mum to her two daughters.

She started writing in her teens, with a love for writing poetry. This soon changed to writing stories for children as she enjoyed reading and sharing tales with the children in her care, and of course her own children too.

Other titles by Clair Maskell:

Mrs Handbag and the Magic Seed

Made in United States
Orlando, FL
12 November 2024